MEET ALL THESE FRIENDS IN BUZZ BOOKS:

The Animals of Farthing Wood
Thomas the Tank Engine
Biker Mice From Mars
James Bond Junior
Fireman Sam
Joshua Jones
Rupert
Babar

First published in Great Britain 1994 by Buzz Books,
an imprint of Reed Children's Books
Michelin House, 81 Fulham Road, London SW3 6RB
and Auckland, Melbourne, Singapore and Toronto

ISBN 1 85591 380 1

Printed in Italy by Olivotto

RUPERT™
and the
GLOW-WORMS

Story by Norman Redfern
Illustrations by SPJ Design

Rupert Bear, Edward Trunk and the Fox
twins were on their way to see the Old
Professor. He had invited them to his tower
to watch a rare display of shooting stars.

"Look!" cried Freddie Fox, as they strolled
through the woods. "Up in the sky! It's a
shooting star!"

"Not yet, Freddie," said Rupert. "We won't
see them until it's dark."

"Well, what's that, then?" asked Freddie.

A golden light was glinting through the
trees in front of them.

"It's coming from the Professor's
window," said Rupert.

He ran to the Professor's tower, but before
he could knock, the door swung open.

"Hello," said the Professor. "Do come in."

Rupert and his friends followed the
Professor up to the top of the tower.

8

"How did you know we were here?"
asked Rupert.

"I was watching for you through my
telescope," said the Professor.

Ferdie Fox raced over to the window and peered through the telescope. The lens caught the evening sun, and a patch of light flickered over the trees.

"Look, Freddie, there's your shooting star," laughed Edward.

"Before you start looking for shooting stars, why don't you see if you can spot some supper?" said the Old Professor. "Star-gazing can be very hungry work, you know!"

Rupert and the Foxes looked eagerly around the Professor's room. Edward sniffed thoughtfully.

"Egg sandwiches!" he cried. "And they're over... there!"

11

As the four friends ate their sandwiches,
the sun set behind the trees. The stars
began to twinkle in the darkening sky.

"Keep your eyes peeled," said the
Professor. "Look towards the pagoda."

12

Rupert, Freddie, Ferdie and Edward
crowded on to the Professor's window-seat.
In the distance they could just see the lights
of Nutwood. All around them was the clear
night sky.

13

"Look!" gasped Rupert.

Like silent fireworks, the shooting stars began flying across the sky. For the next few minutes, the black sky was crossed by tiny bright lights.

The four friends barely blinked as the little stars shot past. But all too soon the display was over.

"Will we see any more?" asked Edward.

"Oh, they'll be back," said the Professor, "but not for many years."

He turned back to the window. A car's
headlights were shining through the trees.

"I think it's time you put on your coats,"
said the Professor.

For a moment, Rupert was puzzled. Then
there was a knock at the Professor's door.

"It's my Daddy," said Rupert. "He's come
to take us home."

Outside the tower, Rupert and Edward thanked the Professor. Freddie and Ferdie were whispering together by the hedge.

"Look, Rupert," said Ferdie, "this is where the shooting stars landed!"

Rupert and Edward ran over to the Foxes. At the bottom of the hedge they could see sparkling lights.

"The shooting stars!" gasped Edward.

Freddie and Ferdie tried not to laugh.

"Those aren't stars," said Rupert. "They're glow-worms! They are pretty, aren't they?"

The Fox twins skipped back to Mr Bear's
car, whispering and giggling as they went.
Behind them, Mr Bear bent down and
picked something up from the ground.

"Hmm, what's this?" he asked Rupert.

"That's Ferdie's watch," Rupert replied.
"If you press a button, it glows in the dark."
  "He must be too busy playing jokes to
notice it's gone," said Mr Bear. "Let's play
a joke on him."

The next day, Rupert asked Edward Trunk and Freddie and Ferdie Fox to come to supper. It was a warm summer's evening, and Mr Bear brought them a bowl brimming with crisp, fresh salad.

"Salad from my own vegetable patch," he said proudly.

The four friends tucked in. Freddie,
Rupert and Edward chatted happily as
they ate, but Ferdie was rather quiet.

"What's the matter?" asked Rupert.

"I've lost my special watch," said Ferdie.
"If you press a button on it, it glows in the
dark. But I can't find it!"

"Don't worry," said Mr Bear. "I'm sure it
will turn up."

After supper, they all helped to wash and
dry the dishes. Then Rupert had an idea.

"It's still warm outside," he said. "Let's
look for glow-worms."

Freddie and Ferdie sighed.

"We saw them yesterday," said Ferdie.

"Come on, you two," said Edward.

Rupert led the way to the garden. He
strolled over to the hedge and knelt down.

"Here they are," he said, pointing.

Edward leant over and looked.

"Yes, and that one's very unusual," he
said. "Come and see, Ferdie."

Ferdie stamped down the path crossly.

"What's so special about it?" he asked.

"Look!" said Rupert.

Ferdie knelt down and peered at the little glowing bugs. There was something strange about one of them. It was glowing, but it wasn't a glow-worm!

"My watch!" he cried.

He picked it up and strapped it tightly on his wrist.

"But how did it get there?" asked Freddie.

Rupert told the Foxes how his father had found it. Then he and Edward had placed it amongst the glow-worms for a trick.

For a moment, Ferdie looked cross. Then he started to laugh.

"That was a good trick, Rupert," he said. "But I'll think of a better one!"

The sky was growing dark and the stars
were glowing brightly. It was time for
Edward, Freddie and Ferdie to go home.

"Goodbye," said Rupert, waving to his
friends. "See you tomorrow."

28

"Thank you for finding my watch, Mr
Bear," said Ferdie.

"You're very welcome," Mr Bear replied.
"It's surprising what good things you can
find in the garden!"